Maureen Haselhurst
Illustrated by Dan Bramall

Chapter 1

Dodge the dig-ups

Baz Boston banged loudly on the front door of Harkback House, but no one could hear him because of the ear-splitting wailing that was going on inside.

He pushed the rusty letter box open. 'Aunt Enna!' he shouted. 'It's me ... '

The wails wheezed into silence and the door was flung open by a bushy-haired young woman, clutching a tattered sack under her arm.

'Hello, Aunt Enna,' said Baz.

She smiled at him vaguely. 'Sorry?'

'It's Baz,' he grinned. 'You know – your nephew.'

'Baz! Oh, I'd forgotten that you were coming.'

Baz shrugged. So what was new? He often stayed with his aunt and she always forgot that he was coming.

'Come on in,' she smiled. 'The house is in a bit of a mess. You'll have to dodge the dig-ups as usual.'

Baz followed her inside. Aunt Enna was an archaeologist with the most bizarre talent for finding anything old and wacky. She called them her dig-ups and the house was bursting with them.

He picked his way along the hall, ducking under the grumpy Mugamoosh witch doctor's mask and hopping over the cute stuffed Australian Wazanozzy.

'What do you think of these?' asked Aunt Enna, holding out the tattered old sack that she'd been clutching.

Baz took it gingerly. It was just a shapeless old bag with five sticks dangling out of it.

'They're the petrifying bagpipes of Wild Hoots McToot,' she told him excitedly. 'I dug them up from a battlefield in Glen Skinchy. Hoots turned the whole of the McLout clan to stone with a single blast. Listen ...'

She stuck one of the sticks between her lips, took a deep breath and blew. The raggedy bag inflated alarmingly and Baz clamped his hands to his ears as a horrendous howl squalled through the house.

Baz made a dash for his bedroom, with his hands still firmly clamped over his ears.

He dropped his backpack onto the bed and looked around the familiar room. Like all the other rooms in Harkback House, it was full of freaky curiosities and dead people's leftovers, but none of them scared him. He had grown up with Hetty the Yeti, standing stuffed and harmless next to his bed. The iron false teeth that had once belonged to a cannibal called Chief Bellibungful were in their usual place on the window sill and the Egyptian sarcophagus was still being used as a wardrobe.

Baz unpacked, hung his clothes in the wacky wardrobe and parked his skateboard in the bottom. He patted Hetty's matted head and smiled; everything was reassuringly crazy. Then, once he was sure that Wild Hoots McToot's bagpipes had run out of puff, he went back downstairs.

Baz wandered into the kitchen to find Aunt Enna upside down in the chest freezer. She was frantically rummaging around in the chaos of frozen pizzas, prawns and bits of mummy wrapped up in cling film.

'Come out, come out wherever you are,' she was cooing playfully. 'I know you're hiding down there.'

Baz watched her suspiciously. That freezer was like the pit of doom. He hadn't forgotten the time she'd taken a shrunken head out of it and very nearly served it up as a Christmas pudding.

'Lost something?' he asked.

Aunt Enna clambered out of the freezer, her bushy hair spiked with frost and prawns.

'Yes. Princess Hedda of Defunctovia,' she said, as if it was perfectly normal to have a princess stuffed away in the icebox. 'Not all of her – just her skull.'

'Why keep a skull in the freezer? It won't go off,' Baz pointed out.

'Oh, but it will,' she contradicted. 'She's still got bits of mummification stuck to her. She'll go mouldy.'

Baz looked squeamish and pulled a 'Bleurgh!' face. 'She'll turn up,' he said trying to steer his aunt away from all the gory details. 'When did you last see her?'

Aunt Enna absent-mindedly picked the prawns out of her hair and began to eat them. 'I'm not sure,' she muttered vaguely. 'I remember having her at the checkout in the supermarket. The girl on the till put her through as a turnip. Pop out and see if I left her in the car will you, Baz?'

Chapter 2
Have dribble – will scribble

Baz sauntered along the winding path that led towards the garage. At every twist and turn, he came face to face with one of Aunt Enna's jumbo dig-ups, plonked down at random amongst the tangle of trees and shrubs. The overgrown garden was like a crazy film set. There were jelly-belly buddhas, bits of toppling temple and marble statues, a fairground helter-skelter, and a steamroller with no steam and no roller. Then came Baz's favourite – an ancient hangman's gibbet that still had its rope.

He took a running jump, grabbed hold of the rope and launched himself out into space.

'Yaaay!' It made a fantastic swing!

He landed at the feet of the most impressive of Aunt Enna's dig-ups. It was a huge stone statue of a cross-eyed god with moss growing out of its ancient nostrils like bushy, green bogies.

Baz set off again, but as he turned the next corner, he stopped in surprise. The garden was covered in ... graffiti!

But this wasn't the usual streetwise graffiti. This graffiti looked like a series of weird puzzles. The walls and paths were covered with wild, silver swirls and curlicues, and curious, complex patterns. It had nothing to do with the dig-ups. It was new and freshly done and it was really, really funky.

'Phew! This is seriously cool stuff,' Baz whistled.

The graffiti was everywhere. It danced along the paths and scampered up steps. It was crazy – it was almost alive!

Baz followed it through the garden, half noticing that something with a big appetite had chomped its way through most of the veggie patch.

Ahead of him, the graffiti changed. It ran up a flight of steps in straight, silver lines that ended in a V shape. They looked almost like ... arrows.

Baz stared. 'They *are* arrows!'

Curiosity got the better of him and, forgetting all about Princess Hedda's skull, he followed them.

At the top of the steps he found another path, coated in some sort of thick, oozy slime. More swirls of silver graffiti rippled out in front of him. But these ones were different. They were joined up. They looked almost like ... writing.

'It *is* writing!' he gasped, and read:

Arty parties
Have dribble, will scribble

Around the next bend, he found another arrow and:

slugart@cooldrool
This way for funky art and arty funk

Buzzing with curiosity, Baz followed the arrow. It led straight towards the garage. Written on a small side door was one word:

GOTCHA!

Taking a deep breath, Baz opened the door.

The dark garage smelt of oil and damp. Aunt Enna's beaten-up old banger was just a badly parked shadow over by the wall. The rest of the place was piled high with boxes of mouldering bits and pieces that had once belonged to dead people.

Baz switched on the torch on his phone. The beam picked out a trail of silver graffiti that wound its way across the concrete floor and up the leg of a broken table.

Without warning, the stillness was broken by a slithering sound.

'Yoo-hoo!' called a jaunty voice.

'Who's there?' squeaked Baz nervously.

Something clattered over there in the darkness. The torchlight shone on to a box on the table that was spilling over with brown, decaying bones. Balanced on top was a battered old skull covered with gleaming, silver graffiti.

Baz groaned. This was typical of Aunt Enna. She might have told him that Hedda could talk! A skull was one thing – a talking skull was out of order.

Just when he thought things couldn't get much stranger – they did. There was a movement inside the skull; a slow, sinister, slithering kind of movement.

Baz swallowed very, very hard. A repulsive tentacle was waving at him out of one of the eye sockets.

'Hey, dude,' it said.

The thing began to ooze out in a black, rubbery roll. On its head were two wriggling stalks and on the end of each stalk was a rotating eyeball. The creature had no arms and no legs; it was just a bulbous belly on a big, flat foot.

Centimetre after centimetre of blubber and slime squirmed over the skull's yellow cheekbones.

Baz felt his skin crawl. The loathsome thing was an oversized, muscle-bound SLUG!

Chapter 3

A talented dollop[1]

The slug was at full stretch now and as burly as a wrestler's arm.

'Sumo's the name, smart-art's the game!' beamed the whopping slug, spraying Baz with slimy spit. 'How's it going, dude?'

Baz dodged out of the way.

'M-my name's Baz, not dude,' he stuttered.

'Well, how's it going, Jazz?' said the slug.

'*Baz,*' Baz corrected him.

'OK, it's *Baz.* Hey, give me a break,' he pouted, drool trickling from the corner of his thick lips. 'Most people would think a talking slug was pretty cool.'

'Well, yes, of course you're cool,' agreed Baz nervously.

'You haven't come to play squash, have you?' demanded Sumo, suspiciously. 'Everybody wants to

[1] a shapeless mass or blob

play squash the slug.'

'Well, *I* don't,' Baz reassured him.

'Whey-hey!' whooped Sumo. 'So, you must have come in answer to my advert.'

Baz looked confused. 'What advert?'

Sumo shimmied his tail and rummaged it around in the box of bones. Eventually, he unearthed a sheet of crumpled newspaper.

'*This* advert,' he said and Baz read:

ARTISTIC PET SEEKS BUDDY

Talented, sleek 'n' chic slug seeks fun-loving buddy.
Must provide plenty of grub.
Follow the arrows and join the queue.
P.S. Nobody with big feet need apply!

'Where's the queue?' asked Baz.

Sumo looked glum. 'There isn't one. Maybe nobody saw the advert.'

Baz smiled at him sadly. So that was what all the arrows and messages on the paths had been about.

'But the good news is that I like you, Baz,' chortled Sumo, cheering up no end. 'So *you* can adopt me.'

'No!' squeaked Baz in alarm. I've come to get that skull. It belongs to my aunt.'

Sumo hunched up crossly. 'No way!' he snorted, spitting a tantrum of drool across the garage. 'This skull's a historic home. I found it and it's findy-keepy[2]. So, it's *mine*!'

He began to inflate. Bigger and bigger he ballooned. His blubbery lips opened like a cavernous keyhole, showing rows and rows of stiletto-style teeth.

'You're just a big bully!' he howled, snivelling like a monstrous baby. 'It's not your auntie's skull. It's *mine*. It's my *home*!'

'OK. We'll sort something out!' yelled Baz.

Sumo clamped his mouth shut. His scowl vanished and he beamed innocently. 'Tell you what, Baz', he said sweetly, 'you can take the skull – but you'll have to take *me* as well. I'll be a brilliant pet.'

'No, you won't!' protested Baz.

Baz had always wanted a pet – but a proper pet, not a blubbery dollop.

'OK, but I'm a talented dollop!' snorted Sumo, reading his mind unnervingly. 'Listen up ... ' and before Baz could stop him, Sumo reared up on his tail and started to recite:

---

[2] finders keepers

'Nobody wants me – you don't, I bet.
Nobody wants a slug for a pet.
Kids love dogs and hamsters,
They love cats and mice.
So what's wrong with a slug?
Why are poor slugs not nice?
I can't catch a stick and I can't give a paw,
But this pet's an artist –
This pet can draw!'

But Baz still wasn't convinced.

'OK, so you're a poet as well, but there's no way you'll make me change my mind,' he said firmly.

Sumo looked grouchy and then shrugged. 'I'm hungry,' he muttered, deliberately changing the subject.

He slithered back inside the eye socket and reappeared with something frayed and brown dangling out of his mouth.

'This skull's an amazing pantry,' he said through a mouthful of whatever-it-was. 'Want some?'

'No thank you,' Baz replied, watching the tail-end of Sumo's dinner disappear into his loose lips.

'Someone's eaten half the garden,' said Baz. 'Was that you?'

'Yup, that was me!' boasted Sumo, belching a burp that reeked of rotten cabbage. 'I'm into mean-green-cuisine. Carnivores! Bleurgh! Fancy eating dead bodies – not me. I'm a total veggie head!'

Baz might have said, *Oh really? You've just scoffed a meat dinner! You've just chewed up what's left of Princess Hedda's mummy!* But he didn't. Instead, he said, 'Well, I'm off. I'll tell my auntie that the skull's busy being a wildlife refuge; she'll be OK with that. Bye Sumo, I hope you get to be somebody's pet soon.'

'Don't worry – I will,' beamed Sumo. 'Yours!'

'I've told you – no way!'

'We could settle it with a joke game,' Sumo suggested innocently. 'The winner takes all.'

'Oh, OK, go on then.' Baz knew loads of jokes.

'And the category is ... ooze jokes,' announced Sumo, and the competition began ...

Sumo: What did the slug say to the parrot?

Baz: Ooze a pretty boy then?

Sumo: What does a slug say when it burps?

Baz: Excooze me.

Sumo: Knock, knock.

Baz: Ooze there.

Sumo: How does a slug feel when it's lost in a maze?

Baz: Er … amoozed? No, wait – that's wrong. It's lost, so it's … confoozed!

Sumo: OK, try this one. What makes a slug fed up?

Baz: Er … um … oh, heck! I give in!

Sumo: LOOZING! Loozing makes a slug fed up. But I'm not a loozer – I've won! Congratulations, Baz. You've got yourself a pet!

Chapter 4

Professor Fogeldurge

They left the garage with Baz carrying Sumo, who was smugly curled up in his historic home.

'How come you can squeeze into there?' Baz wanted to know.

'Because I'm solid muscle,' bragged Sumo. 'I just scrunch up and hey presto – I'm a cute little dollop! Impressive, eh?'

'Very,' agreed Baz. 'And it might be a good idea to stay like that when we get back to the house.'

'Will do,' agreed Sumo happily. 'But let's have a go on the skid-pan[3] first.'

'What skid-pan?' Baz asked.

Sumo waggled his eyeball towards a steep, slimy path. 'That skid-pan,' he said.

It really was a skid-pan! Sumo had laid down a thick slither of ooze that was as smooth and as slippery as ice.

Baz set him down on the ground and within seconds, Sumo had expanded into an oversized dollop again.

'Me first,' he chortled. 'Push me off.'

---

[3] a slippery surface for practising skidding

Baz put the toe of his trainer under Sumo's rear and pushed.

'Yee-ha!' whooped Sumo, standing upright on his tail end and swooping downhill.

'Here I come!' yelled Baz, hurtling after him.

Around the corners they scooted, along the straights they slithered, somersaulting over humps and sliding bellyflap[4] down the other side.

'Yaaay!' cheered Baz, hardly daring to believe that he was having such fun with a slug.

'I told you that I'd be a brilliant pet,' beamed Sumo.

It was ages before Baz got back to Harkback House, carrying his unlikely pet inside Princess Hedda's skull.

An old-fashioned motorbike was parked at the front door.

Sumo burst into a fit of gloopy giggles. 'Take a look at the number plate,' he sniggered.

IMA FOGY

'Try to be serious, Sumo,' Baz warned him. 'We're going in now, so no funny business.'

Sumo crossed his eyes on their stalks and pulled a face. 'OK,' he agreed. 'No funny business.'

'Stay small and stay quiet!'

---

[4] to land or slide on your stomach

'Small and quiet it is, Baz,' hissed Sumo, and he scrunched up into a tight ball.

There were voices coming from the kitchen. Baz popped his head around the door. 'I'm back,' he called.

His aunt looked up expectantly. 'Did you find her?'

'Yes, she was in the garage,' said Baz.

'Excellent. Come and meet Professor Fogeldurge. He runs the Dumpsdown Museum,' she said. 'He's come to see Hoots' bagpipes.'

Professor Fogeldurge was a mushroomy little man, wearing an oddly oversized hat that was way too big for his body. He jumped to his feet, bowed and politely raised his hat to Baz.

'I'm delighted to meet you, young man,' he beamed.

'Now then,' said Aunt Enna, looking around vaguely, 'where did I put Hoots' bagpipes?'

Baz pointed to a saggy tartan bag that was hanging like a tea towel on a hook by the sink. 'I think you were drying the dishes on them,' he said, trying to keep his face straight.

Aunt Enna recovered the bagpipes and tucked them under her arm.

'I'm pretty sure that these are the petrifying pipes

of Wild Hoots McToot of Glen Skinchy!' she told the Professor. 'Shall I give you a tune?' she asked, taking a deep breath.

The Professor looked extremely alarmed, but it was too late. With a dismal moan, the bagpipes howled into action and a gale of screeches and skirls blasted around the kitchen.

Professor Fogeldurge pulled his hat over his ears and dived under the table.

'Stop it! Stop it! I can't stand noise!' he blubbered.

The bagpipes spluttered into silence.

'I have ultra-delicate hearing,' he moaned. 'You should see my earwax. On a bad day, it's the colour of curry.'

Baz pulled a 'Bleurgh!' face.

Professor Fogeldurge clambered back into his chair and examined the bagpipes at arm's length.

'I doubt that Hoots ever tooted this, um, er … artefact. Nobody would give you ten pence for it,' he said, casually spinning a ten pence piece in the air.

Aunt Enna caught it and absent-mindedly dropped it into the toaster instead of the charity box.

'I'm not bothered about how much they're worth,' she said. 'They're not for sale.'

Professor Fogeldurge tapped his nose irritatingly. 'Ah, but everything has its price,' he beamed.

Aunt Enna looked at him crossly. She turned to Baz. 'Thanks for finding Princess Hedda,' she said.

Professor Fogeldurge leapt to his feet.

'Princess ... what princess?' he demanded eagerly, his thin eyebrows disappearing into his hat.

'It's only an old skull,' said Baz hurriedly.

'It is *not*!' retorted his aunt, taking it from Baz. 'It belongs to Princess Hedda of Defunctovia ... and who's been doodling on her?' she asked, prodding the graffiti.

'May I see?' said Professor Fogeldurge, and Aunt Enna passed Hedda over to him. It was like a bizarre game of pass the parcel.

Baz held his breath, silently pleading, *Pleeeease, stay quiet, Sumo!*

The Professor glanced at Hedda's skull dismissively and began to twirl her around on the end of his finger like a basketball.

'The boy is quite right. It's just an old skull. As for the artwork, it's utter tosh! Meaningless scribble!'

Inside his historic home, Sumo was dizzy with fury. He'd had enough. Hedda's skull suddenly jerked in the Professor's hands and a furious voice jeered, 'Quit the jibber-jabber, old fogey-man! You're looking at smart-art. This is the home of Cool Drool!'

Baz groaned. Sumo had blown his cover.

Chapter 5

The incredible Blabbing Baz Boston

The Professor gaped at Hedda.

'My oh my!' he panted, turning pinker than ever. 'It spoke! It's a *talking* skull! This is remarkable. This is the stuff of legend! This changes everything!'

Baz heard himself blurt out, 'It's not a talking skull! It was *me.* I was trying to throw my voice. It was a joke.'

Aunt Enna narrowed her eyes suspiciously.

'I'm sorry about that, Professor,' she apologized. 'It was just Baz being very silly and extremely rude!'

But Professor Fogeldurge totally ignored what she was saying. 'Something as unique as this must be shown to the public,' he said. 'I'll put it on display in the museum.'

He pulled a Dumpsdown Museum carrier bag out of his pocket and slipped Hedda's skull inside.

Aunt Enna looked flustered. 'You've got it all wrong, Professor,' she protested. 'I've had Hedda for years and there's no way that she's a talking skull.'

But Professor Fogeldurge wasn't listening. He gave a quick bow and raised his hat politely.

'Now, I must be going,' he prattled, and hastily gathering up his booty, he trotted out of the house as fast as his plump little legs could carry him.

Baz dashed after him.

'I'm sorry about the joke, Professor. Please give me back the skull. It means a lot to my aunt.'

But it was useless. Pulling his helmet firmly down over his ears, Professor Forgeldurge phut-phutted away on IMA FOGY, with Hedda and his big hat stashed safely in the sidecar. The last Baz heard was Sumo yammering[5], 'Hey, Baz! Get me out of this!'

Baz trailed back into the house. What was he going to do now? He had never wanted a slug for a pet – especially an oversized, blabbermouth of a slug. But Sumo was a talented, funny blabbermouth. Baz couldn't just leave him to a squishy fate. Besides, he fancied another round of ooze jokes.

He found Aunt Enna sitting on the stairs, nursing the stuffed Wazanozzy on her knee.

'Just what are you up to, Baz?' she asked.

'Who, me?' he asked innocently.

'Yes, you. What's all this silly stuff about Hedda

[5] making a loud, repetitive noise

being a talking skull?'

'It was just a joke,' he shrugged.

'And what about the silver doodles on her? Did you do them?'

'No,' he could answer truthfully this time. 'They were there when I found her.'

'Well, they're brilliant!' she said unexpectedly. 'I wonder who did them. I'd like to meet the artist.'

Baz stared at her. Should he tell her? Would she believe him? No, she wouldn't, so he changed the subject.

'I asked geeky old Fogeldurge to give me Hedda back, but he wouldn't,' he told her.

'I suppose he'll bring her back when he realizes that he's wrong and that she can't talk. He gets bats in his hat about things. Anyway, the whole thing is your fault, Baz. That ventriloquist act was very convincing.'

And then she dropped the bombshell.

'You were really good. Do it again!'

Oh heck! Baz dredged his brain for an excuse, but nothing came. Aunt Enna waited patiently on the stairs, picking fleas off the stuffed Wazanozzy.

Baz hadn't the foggiest idea how to throw his voice, but he had to do it – or the whole can of beans would be spilled.

Baz tried to remember exactly what Sumo had said, playing it back through his mind like a mental MP3 player. *Quit the jibber-jabber, old fogey-man! You're looking at smart-art. This is the home of Cool Drool!*

Yes, that was it! All he had to do was imitate Sumo's words without moving his lips – no problem.

Baz climbed up the stairs and stood on the landing. This was it!

'Lady and Wazanozzy,' he announced. 'Here's what you've been waiting for – the world's greatest ventriloquist. The incredible Blabbing Baz Boston!'

Taking a deep breath, he clamped his lips across his teeth and gabbled, 'Git de giller-galler urld ogey-an! Yer ookin a shnartaart. Zis iz de ohm ug oolool!'

Oh no – he'd blown it.

'What a load of mumbo-jumbo! That sounded nothing like Hedda's voice,' Aunt Enna giggled. 'So, if it wasn't you talking – who was it?'

Baz looked shifty. 'Maybe it was somebody leaving a message on my phone,' he suggested lamely.

His aunt stared at him suspiciously. 'And maybe it wasn't. You can't fool me, Baz Boston – you're up to something!'

Chapter 6

Rejects, kaputs and defuncts

Baz sat in his bedroom, trying to get his head around things. Sumo could easily escape from the museum, but he would never leave Hedda behind.

'What would *you* do?' he asked Hetty the Yeti.

Hetty wasn't a real yeti. She was a quarter gorilla, a quarter polar bear, a quarter buffalo and a quarter some-sort-of-alien.

Her glass eyes stared at him vacantly.

'Don't worry about it,' he said and patted her head. 'What I need is ideas,' he muttered and browsed his phone for 'ways to rescue a slug'.

But people didn't seem to do slug rescues. All he found out was:

1. Slugs have one lung and no bones.
2. Slugs have been around since the last Ice Age.
3. Slugs have green blood.
4. Slugs can have up to ninety thousand grandchildren.

'I'm not having ninety thousand pets!' he muttered and switched it off. He was no further forward.

What if the Professor had found Sumo already?

Then he had an even worse thought ... *What if the Professor likes playing squash the slug?*

Baz jumped up as if a fire cracker had exploded under him.

'Hold on, Sumo,' he shouted. 'I'm coming to get you! I don't know how – but I'll do it!'

He had to move quickly. He pulled his skateboard out of the sarcophagus-wardrobe and stuffed Chief Bellibungful's iron false teeth into his pocket as a good luck charm. Then he slipped out of the house and set off to get his pet back.

The skateboard carved its way through the rush hour traffic. Baz sped up the high street and jumped off in front of a grim old building that stood between Bangers and Burgers, and The Hack Shack hair salon.

He didn't know much about the Dumpsdown Museum except that it always came first in the 'Top Ten Places to Miss' competition.

There was a peeling sign on the heavy front door:

DUMPSDOWN MUSEUM

No pets, no cheeky kids, no buggies, no shopping bags, no food, no drink, no music, no phones, no skateboards, NO NOISE!

Picking up his skateboard, Baz went inside and parked it under a hefty oak table in the entrance lobby. He tiptoed into a wide, empty corridor and gazed around the rambling old place.

He had no idea which way to go. What he needed was a map. He was lucky to find one stuffed inside the pouch of a stuffed sort-of-kangaroo, labelled as a Blooeyroo.

A slither of light was showing under a door further along the corridor. The nameplate read:

PRIVATE
Museum Office
NO public admission

By order: Professor Ronald Fogeldurge

Without warning, the door opened. Baz flattened himself into an alcove as the Professor appeared and trotted off along the corridor, his bald head gleaming like a pink balloon. He looked small without his important hat.

Baz heard the heavy front door bang shut and a key rasped in the lock.

Oh no! It must be closing time. Why hadn't he thought about that? Now he was locked inside Dumpsdown Museum!

'Pom-te-pom-te-pom!' warbled the Professor, as he trotted tappy-lappy[6] back into his office. He sounded very pleased with himself about something.

A switch clicked and the lights went out, leaving the echoing museum draped in shadow. Baz groaned. This was going to make finding Sumo even more difficult.

He flicked the torch on his phone and shone it along the corridor. Glimmering in the narrow beam was a series of freshly painted silver arrows. He might have known it – Sumo had left him directions!

---

[6] speedily

'Great!' He did a high-five with a dummy dressed as the not-so-vicious Viking, Blunderoaf Thickthighs.

So, for the second time that day, Baz set off to follow a trail of slimy, sliver arrows, with absolutely no idea where they were taking him.

He didn't have to go far. The arrows stopped at a door labelled 'Rejects, Kaputs and Defuncts'.

Baz quietly pushed the door open. The room smelt of age and rot. 'Sumo?' he whispered. 'Are you in there?'

No reply.

'Stop fooling about.'

No reply.

'OK. I'm coming in!' and Baz stepped inside Rejects, Kaputs and Defuncts.

He immediately wished that he hadn't.

A Mangling-Man-Trap snagged at his ankles, the long, thin claws of a Creeping Clipper Crab combed through his hair and something dangling from the ceiling kept on swatting at him with an enormous trunk.

'I want out!' he yelled.

'No you don't – they're only playing,' a voice piped up. 'So – what kept you, Baz?'

Chapter 7

The knight in shining 'jamas

'Sumo!'

The slug's huge shadow reared up on the wall, like a squidgy black cudgel[7]. It looked strangely threatening.

'Hold it! Keep your distance!' Sumo's voice snapped through the darkness.

'Why?'

'How do I know that you're Baz? You might be old Fogybogysplurge.'

'Well, I'm not,' hissed Baz.

'OK, so answer me this,' sniggered Sumo. 'Where would Baz go to find his pet?'

Baz sighed. 'In a moozeum, I guess,' he said impatiently.

'Whey-hey!' whooped Sumo. 'I knew you'd come to rescue me, Baz.'

He was stretched out across the lid of a large glass case. Inside the case there was something turnipy.

It was a skull.

Hedda! Baz gave a sigh of relief. He had found them both. This was going to be a lot easier than he'd thought.

He gave Sumo a gentle push.

[7] a club-like weapon

'Budge over, so I can get Hedda. Then let's get out of here!'

'No can do,' said Sumo.

'Why?'

'Because, it's not Hedda. It's a fake!'

'This had better not be one of your jokes,' Baz warned him.

A light inside the case suddenly flicked on. There was a label stuck on the glass.

THE TALKING SKULL OF
PRINCESS HEDDA OF DEFUNCTOVIA

FROM TIME TO TIME, THE VOICE OF THE PRINCESS COMES BACK FROM THE DEAD. STAND BACK! DO NOT TOUCH – OR BE CURSED!

There was a faint whirring noise and an eerie voice rose out of the skull.

'Who dares to disturb the sleep of Princess Hedda of Defunctovia? May verrucas sprout between your toes and spiders live inside your nose!'

Baz stared at Sumo in astonishment.

'Don't look at *me,* Baz,' he protested. 'I didn't say a word.'

Baz felt weird. This was unreal.

He slid the lid aside and lifted the skull out. It grinned up at him, discoloured with age and covered in silver swirls and curlicues.

'It looks like Hedda's skull to me,' he said.

'Garbage!' sneered Sumo. 'Check out the graffiti. It's not in my league!'

Baz examined it closely. Sumo was right; it wasn't Cool Drool. It didn't have Sumo's swagger – and it had been done in silver felt-tip pen.

Something inside it rattled. Baz tipped whatever-it-was into the palm of his hand, hoping that it wasn't bits of mummy. It wasn't – it was a tiny MP3 player!

So that was it; the voice was a recording. Come to think of it, it sounded suspiciously like Professor Fogeldurge's squeaky voice.

'You're right. It's a fake,' agreed Baz. 'But it's good enough to fool people.'

He felt around the glass case . His fingers found a tiny button. 'Ah … so that's it! It's controlled by a timer.'

'Oh, phooey to all that techy stuff!' sniffed Sumo dismissively. 'I *knew* it wasn't Hedda. It didn't smell royal and there were no dangly, yummy brown bits to have for elevenses.'

Baz bit his tongue and decided to stay mum about the mummification.

'I want Hedda, Baz!' sniffed Sumo, drool trickling from his eyeballs. 'I want my proper, historic home!'

'We'll find her,' soothed Baz. 'But what's been going on? If there's been a swap, you must have seen it.'

Sumo hung his head. 'I didn't. I wasn't here – at least not all of the time.'

'Just tell me what happened,' said Baz.

Sumo nodded miserably. 'I knew there was something shifty going on. If old Dunglebungle was going to put Hedda on show, then why did he bring her in here with the scrappers?'

Baz nodded.

'He took a quick squint at Hedda's Cool Drool,' Sumo went on, 'and then he laughed and said something like, "Oh yes, my dear, copying you will be a cinch".'

'Then what?'

'That's when the phone rang,' Sumo went on. 'He dumped me and Hedda in the glass case and he dashed off to answer it.'

'Could you hear what he was saying?'

Sumo frowned. 'Not much. All I heard was, "Excellent – I'll see you tonight." I didn't hang about. I wanted to lay the trail for you while the coast was clear.'

'I would have been lost without it,' Baz told him.

Sumo beamed at him. 'I knew that you'd come, Baz. You're my knight in shining 'jamas!'

'It's shining *armour*,' Baz smiled. 'Go on.'

Sumo's flabby mouth flopped sadly. 'When I got back, the fake skull was in the case and Hedda had gone.'

'And you're sure that Professor Fogeldurge didn't see you?' asked Baz.

'Sure. I was in a Supreme-Sumo-Scrunch-Up,' he boasted.

'So, what's he up to?' muttered Baz – and then he remembered something that the Professor had said to Aunt Enna: *Everything has its price* ...

'Got it!' he gasped. 'He's going to put the fake Hedda on show, so that he can sell the real Hedda. And he's going to do it tonight!'

Chapter 8

The Mean Dream Team

'Run that past me again, Baz,' said Sumo.

'OK. Professor Fogeldurge made a fake skull and swapped it for the real Hedda,' explained Baz again. 'He thinks that she's worth a whole heap of money because she's a rare talking skull.'

'But she's not!' blustered Sumo. 'She's a class act, but she doesn't do talking. I should know – she's never chatted *me* up!'

'*I* know that, but he heard *your* voice coming out of *her* skull and he's convinced that she's genuine,' Baz insisted.

'So what's he done with her?' demanded Sumo.

'If he plans to sell her tonight, I guess she'll be in his office,' said Baz.

'Well, let's go and rescue her,' gabbled Sumo. 'A boy and his pet,' he beamed. 'Hey, Baz, we're a Mean Dream Team!'

The Mean Dream Team's job seemed simple enough. Find Hedda's skull and take it back to Harkback House, without bumping into Professor Fogeldurge while they were doing it.

The museum was shrouded in shadows and was as silent as a graveyard.

'It's very quiet – are you sure that the Professor's still here?' whispered Baz, as he and Sumo glided silently along the corridor towards the museum office.

'Yup. I can smell him.'

'You haven't got a nose,' Baz pointed out.

'Who needs a nose?' snorted Sumo. 'I smell with my foot.'

Baz sniffed. 'Pooh! I can smell your foot as well.'

'I said that I smell *with* my foot!' repeated Sumo. 'If I looze my way and I get the blooze, it choozes a trail and ... ' he stopped, running out of ooze jokes.

'That's interesting nooze and I refooze to looze this round of ooze jokes!' chuckled Baz triumphantly.

Sumo hunched up in a huff. He hated losing. But Sumo's sulk was cut short by the sound of a loud knocking on the front door of the museum.

'Oh no!' hissed Baz. 'It's starting already ... '

He yanked Sumo behind Blunderoaf Thickthighs as the office door opened and a beam of light shafted along the dark corridor. Professor Fogeldurge hurried out of his office, smiling from one small pink ear to the other.

'Keep calm, Ronald,' he chuntered[8] to himself. 'That's royalty knocking at your door – even if he is ex-royalty. Ex-King Dudley of Defunctovia,' he sniggered. 'But who cares if he's a dud – so long as he's got the dosh!'

And, rubbing his chubby, pink hands together, he scurried off towards the front door.

Baz nudged Sumo urgently. 'This is it. Here's our chance to get Hedda's skull back. Go, go, go!'

Sumo reared up and slithered across the shiny wooden floor and into the museum office with Baz hot on his tail.

It was a stuffy old-fashioned room, piled high with a hotchpotch of unidentifiable odds and ends, but Hedda was not one of them.

Then ...

'Found her!' whooped Sumo, whirling around on his tail end in excitement.

Lying, upside down, on the desk was the Professor's oversized hat. It looked remarkably like a large black nest and snuggled inside the nest was what looked like a large brown egg.

'Home, sweet home,' Sumo chortled and he slithered back into his historic home and scuffled around in the familiar nooks and crannies.

---

[8] grumbled

'Stop fooling around and let's get out of here,' said Baz.

But ... clack, clack, clack – two sets of footsteps were coming along the corridor and heading straight for the office. They were cornered.

'Keep your head down!' Baz hissed to Sumo. 'We've both got to stay out of sight – or it's all over!'

Chapter 9

Blingking Dud of Defunctovia

Standing in one corner of Professor Fogeldurge's office was a tall, wooden screen. Baz squeezed himself behind it and put his eye to a knot hole, just as Professor Fogeldurge and his visitor came into the office.

The Professor stood behind his desk, looking small and pink and pompous. On the other side of the desk was a tall, showy man wearing designer jeans, a white leather jacket and a whole lot of jewellery. He wore several bracelets, a couple of watches and a necklace as thick as a rope. And every bit of it was made of shining, yellow gold.

'The Dumpsdown Museum is proud to welcome you, ex-King Dudley,' purred the Professor.

'Just call me Dud,' drawled the ex-King. 'I got sacked from being a proper king, but I was lucky to have a royal fortune stashed away. The only kind of king I am nowadays is a *bling* king,' he said, rattling his gold jewellery. 'Blingking Dud!'

Professor Fogeldurge looked blank. He didn't do jokes.

'Excellent!' beamed the Professor. 'Now then, er, Dud, I believe that you collect rare antiquities. I think you might be interested in this,' and he lifted Hedda's skull out of his hat.

Blingking Dud looked horrified and leapt backwards. 'That's not a rare antiquity!' he yelled. 'That's a monstrosity! Why should I be interested in a decaying old skull?'

'Because this is the skull of your great, great ... (Baz counted at least a dozen more 'greats') ... grandmother, Princess Hedda of Defunctovia,' cooed the Professor.

'So what?' shrugged ex-King Dud.

Professor Fogeldurge smirked. 'This is the stuff of legend,' he whispered mysteriously. 'This is a *talking* skull. Your great, etcetera, etcetera, grandmother speaks. I myself have heard her.'

Blingking Dud stared at him suspiciously. 'I don't believe in the talking dead, Professor,' he sneered. 'I'm not interested.'

But Professor Fogeldurge didn't give up that easily.

'Why don't you examine it?' he suggested, thrusting Hedda into Blingking Dud's hands.

'Quit it, Professor!' he shouted. 'I don't want to

examine the rotten thing! It's all stuck up with slime. It's trash. Bin it!' And he tossed Hedda's skull into the waste paper basket. 'I'm off!'

'Good riddance, dude!' jeered a voice.

Blingking Dud stopped in his tracks and glowered at Professor Fogeldurge. 'There's no need to be rude!' he snapped.

The Professor's pink face turned white. 'But I didn't say a word!'

Behind the screen, Baz groaned. Silly Sumo! Why couldn't he keep his sluggy mouth shut? He'd ruined everything – again.

Blingking Dud picked Hedda out of the bin. 'Well, hi there, Great Grandmother,' he drawled. 'Maybe you *are* a talking skull after all.'

'Now do you believe me?' asked Professor Fogeldurge.

'Maybe. How much do you want for it?' asked Dud, casually tossing Hedda from one hand to the other, like a bony ball.

The Professor named a huge amount of money.

'How much?' gasped ex-King Dud.

The price was so enormous that he missed his catch and Hedda went stotting[9] across the floor.

---

[9] bouncing

'Ouch! Clumsy clot!'

Professor Fogeldurge smirked triumphantly. There could be no doubt now. The skull had spoken – twice.

Blingking Dud picked Hedda up and placed her gently on the desk.

'Awesome!' he gasped, his eyes lighting up greedily. 'OK, Professor, I'm convinced. It's unique. It's the eighth wonder of the world – and I've got to have it!'

'The price has just gone up,' Professor Fogeldurge informed him craftily.

'Whatever it takes,' agreed Blingking Dud. 'Meet me at the Quidsin Bank at noon tomorrow and I'll give you the dosh.'

As soon as the two men had left the office, Sumo slithered out of Hedda's skull and appeared around the screen.

'I guess I blew it again,' he said.

'Too right you did!' growled Baz. 'Let's grab Hedda and get out of here.'

But it was too late; Professor Fogeldurge skipped back into his office, hugging himself.

'Money, money, money!' he sang. 'I'm going to be *rich*!'

He picked up Hedda's skull and gave it a pulpy kiss. 'Now then, my priceless Princess,' he crooned, 'let's put you away safely', and he popped her into a stout iron safe and locked her in.

'Bring on noon, tomorrow!' he chuckled. 'Or should that be, *bling* on noon, tomorrow? Gosh – I think I've just made a joke!'

Then, pulling on his oversized hat, he scampered off. The museum door banged closed, a key rasped in the lock and an engine phut-phutted away.

'Great!' said Baz sarcastically. 'Hedda's locked up in the safe and we're locked up in the museum.'

Chapter 10

The Phut Mutts

'What next, Baz?' asked Sumo, as the two of them wandered aimlessly around the deserted museum.

'We go home,' said Baz.

'It's all right for you,' sulked Sumo. '*My* home's locked up in here. I'm not going anywhere without it!'

Baz was tired and fed up. 'Tough!' he retorted. 'Your home's locked up because you couldn't keep your flabby mouth shut!' and he stalked off angrily.

'Hold it! Where are you going?' called Sumo.

'To look for a way out of this dump!'

Sumo pulled a sulky face behind Baz's back, but he cheered up when he spotted an apple core rotting under a radiator.

'I've found a scrummy deli, for my empty little belly!' he burbled and got down to some serious chomping.

Baz hurried through the dismal building, but everything was securely locked.

He had to face it – there was no way out.

'I thought you'd gone home!' grunted Sumo when Baz came back.

'I can't find a way out,' Baz admitted, flopping down beside him.

Sumo looked huffy. 'You were dead mean to me,' he pouted.

'Yes. I'm sorry.'

'So, am I still your pet?' lisped Sumo, pathetically.

Baz smiled. 'I suppose so.'

'Great!' beamed Sumo. 'Because I've had an ace idea about how to get Hedda back.'

'How?' asked Baz without much interest.

'We're going to crack the safe!'

Baz stared at him in amazement. 'That's a seriously daft idea.'

'Not when you've got the know-how,' said Sumo.

Baz raised his eyebrows doubtfully.

'I hatched out in a burglar's swag bag,' announced Sumo proudly. 'I learned all the tricksy-tricks of the trade when I was just a dinky little squidge.'

'What did you burgle?' asked Baz.

'Posh nosh,' said Sumo proudly. 'Cabbages, lettuces, cucumberumbers ...'

'All slugs do that,' said Baz dismissively. 'Do you *really* know how to crack a safe?'

'You bet,' nodded Sumo. 'We blow it up!'

Baz shook his head. 'You need explosives to blow things up.'

'So you do,' agreed Sumo and he sniggered. 'Guess what I found when you were looking for a way out? Come on, follow me!'

'I don't think I want to see this,' groaned Baz and he followed Sumo through the fusty museum.

'Pssst! In here!' Sumo hissed, swerving into an open door. 'Meet the Phut Mutts[10],' he grinned.

Baz looked around. Five dummies, with various bits missing, were slumped around a wooden barrel. They were wearing frilly shirts and the ones that still had their heads wore floppy hats. On the wall was a sign:

The Failure of the Gunpowder Plot

'Gimme a bang! Gimme a boom!' chortled Sumo, 'and hey presto – we've cracked the safe!'

Baz peered into the open barrel. It was half full of a dry white powder. It couldn't really be gunpowder – could it? No, surely not.

'I've got no idea what this stuff is,' he told Sumo. 'It could be really dangerous. Let's forget it!'

[10] foolish plotters in a failed plan

'But if we don't get Hedda back tonight, I'll have lost my home forever,' murmured Sumo dejectedly.

'OK, let's do it,' Baz agreed reluctantly.

But it wasn't that easy. The barrel was very big and very heavy.

'We'll have to take the gunpowder a bit at a time,' said Baz. 'We need a bag or something to carry it in.'

There were no bags, but they found some old socks in a room called Laundry Through the Ages. They would have to do.

Backwards and forwards Baz tramped, carrying the dangerous bundles that might explode at any moment.

'This is taking far too long,' he told Sumo. 'I'm going to try rolling the barrel.'

'What you need is a skid-pan,' babbled Sumo eagerly and he slid off at full stretch with his foot drooling a wide slither of slime.

Baz put the lid on the barrel, heaved it onto its side and pushed. Off it lurched, lazily booling[11] along the corridor until it reached the skid-pan. Then it slipped, slithered, accelerated and it was off!

Along the corridor it bowled, orbiting obstacles and bouncing down steps. Faster and faster it rolled,

---

[11] bowling/rolling

cruising around corners, zipping along straights and somersaulting down ramps.

Baz grabbed Sumo and hurtled after it.

'If that stuff really is gunpowder, it'll explode if it hits anything!' he panicked.

He caught up with the barrel and then dived in a spectacular rugby tackle. He sprawled across it, his feet braking against the floor. There was a clatter as the lid sprang off. The barrel swerved out of control and spun wildly along the corridor with Baz hanging on for dear life.

There was the sound of splintering wood as the barrel smashed into the wall and fell apart like the segments of an orange.

Baz clamped his hands to his head and waited for the explosion.

Chapter 11

Dodge the ghoul drool

There was a long silence and then, 'Yoo-hoo, Baz,' said Sumo, peeling Baz's hands from his face.

Baz peered around. Everything was white. White shimmered in the air. A white Sumo slithered over his own white hand like a whopping, white ghost.

Baz tried to say something but his mouth was clogged with white powder. He panicked and spat out a mouthful.

'Hey, great spitting, Baz,' joked Sumo, dribbling white drool down his chest. 'Let's have a spitting contest.'

'Quit the funny stuff, Sumo,' he snapped. 'This stuff isn't gunpowder after all – it's flour!'

He clambered to his feet and stood knee deep in shattered wood and drifts of flour.

'Got any more good ideas?' he asked Sumo.

For once, Sumo had nothing to say.

'We need to get cleaned up,' said Baz. 'There's a washroom over there. Coming?'

Sumo didn't seem too keen.

'I don't do washing,' he sniffed. 'I just do drool and ooze.'

'Please yourself,' shrugged Baz and he strode off into the washroom.

Baz was rinsing his face in a cracked washbasin when Sumo started to yell. 'Get yourself out here, Baz! We've got a ghost! I've cornered a ghoul!'

Baz sprinted out of the washroom. 'What's going on? What the *heck* is going on?'

Sumo was bouncing around on his tail end, like a heavyweight boxer. He was still smeared in a thick white paste of flour and slime that made him look like an oversized roll of lardy pastry.

He was eye-to-eye with another bulky, white, writhing dollop.

'Come on then, freaky-face,' he jeered, fiercely brandishing his eyestalks. 'Let's play dodge the ghoul drool!' And he puckered up his flabby lips.

'Leave it!' Baz warned, but he was too late.

Sumo shot out a spray of drool. It hit something solid and splashed back, hitting him in the face.

'Hey – that ghoul packs a mean spray,' scowled Sumo.

'That's because it isn't a ghoul – it's *you*! You're looking in a mirror.'

Sumo slithered backwards and admired his doughy reflection in the tarnished mirror.

'Wow! I'm mega soggy!' he crowed excitedly. 'Hey, I can do smart-art and *clart-art*[12] now!'

'Forget it,' Baz told him. 'What you need is a bath ...'

A few minutes later, Sumo was in the washbasin, up to his eyeballs in bubbles.

'I guess I goofed with the Gunpowder Plot,' he admitted. 'Don't worry Baz, I'll come up with another plan,' and he slithered under the bubbles.

Baz wandered out into the empty corridor and slumped down onto a sagging chair labelled 'The Throne of Emperor Pootle the Loafer'. He closed his eyes and began to talk the problem over with himself.

Baz: This is crazy. I'm stuck in this dump so that my pet slug can get his historic home back.

Baz's Brain: Normal people don't have a slug for a pet and normal slugs don't live in historic homes.

Baz: Maybe not, but that's the way it is.

Baz's Brain: But the skull's locked away. Why hang around?

Baz: So that my pet slug can get his historic home back.

And so he went round in circles.

[12] messy art or art made from a sticky mess

Baz's Brain: If the Professor's up to no good, you should tell the police.

Baz: No one's going to believe a boy and a slug.

Baz's Brain: That means other people need to know what's going on.

Baz opened his eyes. That was it! If other people knew about the con, then they would tell the police.

Baz: But what happens if nobody turns up tomorrow morning?

Baz's Brain: You'll have to make sure that they do. Do something to grab their attention. You could try changing this dump into the wackiest place in town!

Baz did a high five in the mirror. 'Brilliant!' he chortled and, pulling the museum map out of his pocket, he started to write on the back.

The Plan

Phase 1

Sumo covers museum in graffiti for Cool Drool impact.

Baz collects materials for wacky displays.

Phase 2
Sumo writes funk-art banner headlines exposing Prof F's dirty tricks.
Baz puts wacky displays together.

Phase 3
Baz transfers fake skull to eye-catching position in display area.
Sumo lays down arrow trail leading to fake skull.
Baz writes visitor blurb, exposing Prof F's fake skull.

Phase 4
Sumo and Baz find hidey-hole and watch the action.

'Sumo!' shouted Baz. 'Get out of the bath. We've got work to do!'

Sumo rinsed himself under the hot tap while Baz talked through the plan with him.

'I like it, I like it, I like it!' chortled Sumo.

'Yeah, it's a good plan,' smiled Baz.

'Plan? Oh, I wasn't meaning the plan, I was talking about *me*!' said Sumo, admiring his squeaky clean reflection in the mirror. 'Hey, I'm as smooth and lean as a stick of liquorice.'

'Are you up for this or not?' demanded Baz. 'It's the only way you're going to get your home back.'

'Of course I'm up for it!' said Sumo. 'But there's a tiddly little problem.'

'What?'

'I've got a tight schedule and slugs can't speed. What I need is transport!'

Baz tugged at his hair. Why hadn't he thought about that?'

'Come on,' he said. 'We'll have to find you a set of wheels.' And slinging his pet across his shoulders, he set off in search of a slugmobile.

'Hey, get this! I'm a proper pet,' crowed Sumo. 'I'm having a carry!'

Chapter 12
The Slugmobile

Baz set off in search of a slugmobile with Sumo riding on his shoulders like a thick rubber tyre.

They found exactly what they wanted in a room called Vintage Vehicles. There, half hidden among the rotting carts and rusting trailers was …

'A dodgem car!' they whooped.

'We've got wacky wheels!' chortled Sumo excitedly.

The dodgem was dunched[13] and dented, but it had four wheels, a steering wheel and a horn.

'What are you waiting for?' asked Sumo. 'Let's roll!'

Baz didn't need to be told twice. He jumped into the driving seat and pushed the foot pedals. They were stiff with age, but gave in to the pressure. The dodgem juddered and then jerked forward. They were on the move.

Baz forgot about everything; he forgot about Hedda, about the Professor and about the plan. Nothing mattered except the thrill of driving the dodgem car through the winding corridors, with Sumo riding pillion, yelling, 'Give it more gas, Baz!'

[13] damaged

They screeched around a corner, narrowly missing a suit of armour that had once belonged to Sir Jouster Thwack.

'Hit the horn, Baz!' yelled Sumo.

Baz hit the horn. But this was no ordinary hooting horn. This horn punched out pre-recorded sound bites.

'Get outta the way, road hog!' it heckled.

'Wow, it doesn't hoot – it hollers,' chortled Baz and he hit it again.

'What the heck was that manoeuvre?' bawled the horn. 'Blow yer rootin' tootin' scooter hooter!'

'My turn to drive ...' grinned Sumo, as the dodgem came to a halt. 'But I can't,' he remembered, and his smile faded. 'No arms, no legs ...' He slithered back onto Baz's shoulders.

'But we can still use it,' Baz pointed out. 'I'm going to have to carry really heavy stuff. I can hook up the dodgem to one of those trailers – and I'm sorted.'

'Yeah – *you're* sorted, but what about me?' pouted Sumo.

He was right. They needed to get Sumo his wheels, but everything needed arms and/or legs, except ...

' ... *of course*! How come I forgot all about *that*?' muttered Baz. 'Come on, Sumo, let's get you your wheels.'

Baz's skateboard was exactly where he had left it, under the table in the entrance lobby.

'Here you are,' he said. 'Meet the Slugmobile.'

Sumo stared at it. He was seriously disappointed. 'It's just a plank on wheels,' he grumbled.

'Yes, but watch.' Baz jumped onto the board and scorched off down the corridor.

Sumo watched, awestruck, as the board leapt up under Baz's feet with its wheels in the air.

'That's called air-riding,' shouted Baz.

He carved around the corner, flipped the board in the opposite direction and then rolled backwards towards Sumo.

'And that was a heelflip followed by a fakie.'

Sumo cheered up no end.

'It looks easy enough,' he said and confidently flexed his blubbery body. He wriggled his big, flat foot onto the board and began to roll forward.

'Hey, I'm croozing!' he chortled. 'I'm a natch! This is a cracking bit of kit. Let's move it, Baz – we've got a historic home to save!' And off he scooted to give the gloomy old Dumpsdown Museum some Cool Drool oomph.

Baz hooked up the best of the Vintage Vehicles'

trailers to the back of the dodgem. He needed to do a sweep of the whole building for weird and wonderful stuff.

He checked out the museum map.

DUMPSDOWN MUSEUM	
Room 1	The Downfall of a Dynasty
Room 2	Historical Bathroom Devices
Room 3	Vintage Vehicles
Room 4	Bones – a History of Death
Room 5	North American Indian Hobbies
Room 6	The Art of Mummification
Room 7	The Failure of the Gunpowder Plot
Room 8	Laundry Through the Ages
Room 9	The Disaster of Modern Music

'It all sounds deadly dull. No wonder hardly anybody comes here,' said Baz as he jumped into the dodgem's driving seat. 'Let's hope we can find some interesting stuff somewhere.'

This was it then. He was ready to roll! He suddenly felt charged with energy. They had to stir things up, big time – and it all had to be done tonight!

Chapter 13

A whole heap of shock factor

Baz drove the dodgem into the entrance lobby. Sumo had been at work in there already and had covered the walls with startling, silver graffiti.

'That looks great.' grinned Baz. 'I need to put something really jokey at the front door to grab people's attention and get them in here.'

'Yup. Let's put the frights up old Funglejungle!' laughed Sumo and he zipped off on the Slugmobile, singing at the top of his voice and way out of tune.

'Wish me luck!' shouted Baz.

He pushed the dodgem's pedals and off he went in search of anything odd and freaky that took his fancy.

It didn't really matter where he started, so he turned into The Downfall of a Dynasty. The Downfall display had mostly fallen down. However, Baz spotted a couple of frayed dummies busy having their heads cut off. They were labelled 'Victims of the Yoo-Stin-Ki Dynasty'.

Baz grinned as he heaved the unfortunate Yoo-Stin-Ki onto the trailer. He'd just had a great idea what to do with them.

He stopped off to gather the washing line and what was left of the socks from Laundry Through the Ages, a large Victorian potty from Historical Bathroom Devices and the dummy of the not-so-vicious Viking, Blunderoaf Thickthighs.

The trailer was piled high by now. Baz drove it back to the canteen and started to unload it in there. It seemed the best place to use as a base.

'How goes it, Baz?' called Sumo, wildly whizzing around him at a dizzying speed. 'I've finished in here. I reckon it's a masterpiece of groovy graffiti!' he boasted and, with a nifty heelflip, he carved off to work his magic in the corridor.

Baz laughed and hit the dodgem's horn. 'What the heck was that manoeuvre?' it yelled.

Baz's next call was in Bones – a History of Death. The room was a shambles of shattered bones and fossils. They were all a bit creepy, but what he wanted was something that had a whole heap of shock factor – and he found it!

The huge skeleton stood upright. It had a mouthful of jagged teeth and a long jointed tail. But that was where the resemblance to an animal stopped.

Instead of front legs, it had curved bones that could have been handles. Even stranger was that where its back legs should have been, there were two huge, bony discs. This creature had moved on wheels!

Baz read the label:

Bicyclaurus: Primitive Wheeled Dinosaur

Phew, what a find!

'I bet it's one of old Fogelsplurge's fakes,' grunted Sumo as Baz unloaded it.

'Maybe,' agreed Baz. 'Even so, it's pretty mind-blowing.'

It was then that they heard the banging ... someone was thumping on the front door!

'Security!' yelled a hoarse voice. 'What's going on in there?'

The razor sharp beam of a torch stabbed through the letter box.

'Stand back Baz,' blustered Sumo. 'I'll zap him with a blast of mega drool!'

'No, you won't! Leave this to me,' hissed Baz. 'We've got to bluff it out.'

'Open the door,' grunted Mr Security.

'No can do,' said Baz, dropping his voice as low as he could. 'We're locked in. We've lost the keys.'

'State your name and business,' growled Mr Security.

'Spic 'n' Span Painting Services,' said Baz. 'Overnight make-overs are our speciality.'

'Oh yeah? Gimme proof,' heckled Mr Security.

'Check it out through the letter box,' said Baz and he stood aside.

The letter box opened and a pair of dark glasses peered in.

'Phew, you guys do seriously cool stuff,' whistled Mr Security, staring at Sumo's Cool Drool graffiti on the lobby walls. 'OK. Carry on. Sorry for troubling you.'

Chapter 14

Whey-hey for the U.S. of A.

Sumo and Baz waited, statue still, as the heavy boots clomped away.

'That was awesome, Baz!' breathed Sumo. 'That was off-the-cuff-bluff at its best.'

Baz looked relieved. 'Well Mr Spic and Mr Span have got an overnight make-over to do,' he smiled. 'So let's do it!' And off he drove to see what he could find in North American Indian Hobbies.

According to the exhibit, the North American Indians' favourite hobby was leaping over tepees. Grinning cheekily from a corner was a life-size cardboard cut-out of a famous tepee-leaper, called Little Leepytepee. Next to him was the actual Tiptop Totem Pole that he had won at the US of A Totempolympics.

'Whey-hey for the U.S. of A.' laughed Baz and he loaded them into the trailer.

He picked up a burly Roman gladiator called Bashius Maximus and then the mouldering mummy of Queen Wannabee the First, who didn't seem to be having a bundle of fun in The Art of Mummification. They were both just perfect.

Baz collected the Gunpowder Phut Mutts and pulled over to give Sir Jouster Thwack a lift. He picked up a plastic crocodile puppet from a derelict Punch and Judy booth and a selection of stuffed animal heads from the walls.

This would be his last load, so he decided to have some fun with the dodgem.

'Hold on in the back!' he shouted to his curious collection of passengers and he pushed mega hard on the pedals.

The accident was his fault. He misjudged a corner and slammed into something big and hard. The impact threw him out of his seat and sent him skidding across the wooden floor. He winced as he pulled a spelk[14] out of his knee, then limped over to inspect the damage.

The victim was a tall box, half hidden under a mangy bearskin rug. The top of the box was glass, and inside were rows of shiny black discs and a turntable. Along the front panel was a row of chunky plastic dials. Baz chose the red one and twiddled it ...

There was a flicker and a series of gaudily coloured bulbs flashed into life. He twiddled another dial.

---

[14] a splinter

A metal grabber stretched forward, picked up one of the discs and dropped it onto the turntable. A guitar twanged, a cymbal crashed and a woman's voice belted out:

'Gimme a rock 'n' roll!
Gimme a twist and shout!
Gimme a jumpin' jive
and we'll shake it all about!'

Wow! Baz twiddled the dials again. The lights flickered off and the music stopped.

He stepped back and looked at the wonderful box. Written in faded red and gold lettering was 'Jive with the Juke'. It was a jukebox – and it worked!

A few minutes later, Baz arrived back at base and unloaded the last of his wacky collection.

'Funky junk!' said Sumo admiringly.

They grinned at one another.

'Well, that's Phase 1 complete,' said Baz. 'Now for Phase 2: I put the displays together while ace reporter Sumo spreads the news.'

Sumo's eyeballs twizzled around excitedly on their stalks. 'Baz builds wacky wonders and Sumo dishes the dirt!' he chortled.

'You got it!' agreed Baz.

Chapter 15
Cool Drool and arty facts

Baz had lost all sense of time; he checked his phone.

'I don't believe it, the battery's dead!' he muttered.

'There's a clock over there, but it's a no-hoper,' said Sumo, wagging his eyestalks towards a lopsided grandfather clock with no hands.

'Well, it's still dark outside, so I guess we've got time to get everything done,' said Baz hopefully.

He ran his eyes over the weird cast of characters and all his other bizarre finds. He'd got some very promising material, but what was he going to do with it?

'I need inspiration,' he told Sumo.

'You got it – here I am,' Sumo chortled.

'Be serious, Sumo,' muttered Baz.

'I *am* being serious. I'm an artist. I *oooooze* inspiration!'

'I'm sorry, go on then – what's your idea?'

'Think jumbo, topsy-turvy dig-ups ...' began Sumo.

'Aunt Enna's garden! It's like a crazy film set! That's exactly the kind of thing I need to make. Thanks Sumo – you're the biz!'

'I know,' grinned Sumo smugly.

Baz smiled. Could they really turn this frumpy old place into a gobsmacking, mind-boggling, jaw-dropping experience, and get it done before Professor Fogeldurge came back?

You bet they could!

All through the night the museum echoed with hoots of laughter, as Baz and his pet raced harum-scarum through the gloomy building.

The skateboard purred along the corridor with Sumo standing on the board at full stretch. Every now and then, he screeched to a halt and slithered up a wall or along a ceiling. Then he would glide back to his Slugmobile, leaving behind him the stunning banner headlines that would dish the dirt on Professor Ronald Fogeldurge's nasty little game.

The dodgem car clanked to and fro with its hollering hooter bawling and the trailer groaning under the weight of its curious cargo. Little by little, Baz's bizarre creations took shape and little by little, the pile on the canteen floor got smaller.

By the time they had finished, the first fingers of sunlight were sliding into the dim museum. Now they could see what they'd done.

It was mind-blowing!

The museum walls, ceilings and floors were covered in a fantastical display of Sumo's trademark graffiti. Scattered amongst it were huge, silver banner headlines:

OOZE NOOZE

TOFF PROF IN DODGY DEAL

FOGEY MAN'S A BOGEYMAN!

LOOK OUT! DODGY DEALER ABOUT!

WHOOZE A BIG CHEAT THEN?

It was like no other art exhibition there had ever been in the world.

'I sure do impressive stuff,' bragged Sumo. 'Now let's check out yours, Baz.'

Baz held up the new exhibition plan.

Cool Drool and Arty Facts

A cast of curious characters from:

1. 21st Century Yoo-Stin-Ki Dynasty
2. Whey-hey for the U.S. of A.
3. Glad to be a Gladiator
4. Fun with the Pharoahs
5. Gunpowder Phut Mutts
6. The Shock of the Sock

Baz's wild and wacky happenings were wilder and wackier than anything in Aunt Enna's crazy garden.

In the entrance lobby, Sir Jouster Thwack was sitting on the top of the totem pole, wearing a large Victorian potty on his head.

The beheaded Yoo-Stin-Kis were in the canteen, hungrily pushing pizzas down their necks. A crowd of stuffed animal heads were gossiping at another table, while their stuffed bottoms were hung along the walls instead.

Under festoons of bunting made from the Shock Socks, Bashius Maximus was threatening the posse of Phut Mutts with the crocodile puppet. Close by, Blunderoaf Thickthighs was playing leapfrog with Little Leepytepee and the Bicyclaurus was doing a nifty wheelie, with the Blooeyroo riding on its back.

Finally, there was a special surprise for Professor Fogeldurge. Spinning around in his office chair was the mouldy mummy of Queen Wannabee the First!

'Now for Phase 3,' said Baz. 'And everything depends on us getting this one just right!'

Chapter 16
Chief Bellibungful bites again!

They drove off to Rejects, Kaputs and Defuncts in the dodgem car. Baz lifted the glass case containing the fake Hedda onto the trailer and drove it back to the wacky display area.

He offloaded the case onto a table in the middle of the weird displays, while Sumo laid a trail of slimy, silver arrows that led towards it.

'All we have to do now is the rest of the headline splashes and the blurb to go on the case, then we're finished,' said Baz. 'We need to get a move on.'

'Hey, trust me, Baz,' swaggered Sumo. 'These headlines are gonna be gutsy! They're gonna be punchy! They're gonna have *oomph*!'

'Just get on with it,' laughed Baz.

Sumo slithered up the wall behind the glass case and drooled in his startlingly bold writing:

SKULL SLUGGERY BREAKING NOOZE!

RON'S A CON!

LOOK OUT - SKULLNAPPER ABOUT!

IT'S A HOAX - IT'S A FIDDLE - IT'S A FIX!

TALKING SKULL A SWIZZ!

'Has that got attitude or has that got attitude?' he called down to Baz.

'If *you've* done it, it's got to have attitude,' said Baz shortly.

He was getting twitchy. It was broad daylight outside now and it must be nearly opening time. He had to get the blurb written before it was too late. He chewed the end of his pen thoughtfully and then wrote:

Urgent information – please read this!

You are being conned! This talking skull is a fake. Press button under lid to activate hidden MP3 player.
The genuine skull is being sold to a wealthy buyer today.
Name of conman: Professor Ronald Fogeldurge.

P.S. The genuine skull can't talk either, but it belongs to somebody who really misses it.

Then he stuck it onto the lid of the glass case.

'Phew, done it!' he whistled. 'All we have to do now is hide and watch what happens.'

He suddenly felt nervous. Had they forgotten anything? He took a last look around.

Everything was there; the graffiti, the headlines, the crazy displays, the arrow trail and the fake Hedda – right in the middle of things where people just had to see her. All that was missing were the people.

Well, they had done their best. They had laid the bait. Now it was up to other people to take it.

'OK. It's time for you and me to lie low,' he told Sumo. 'We need to disappear.'

The grizzly bearskin rug was flopped down on the canteen floor. Baz deliberately hadn't used it yet, but it had a very important role to play in the plan – it was going to make Baz and Sumo vanish.

Baz dragged it into a shadowy corner where they could watch the action. 'Come on, under we go,' he told Sumo.

And giggling with excitement, they wriggled into hiding.

The grizzly bearskin was a bit smelly, but they got a great view through its gaping jaws.

'Drat! It won't stay fastened,' muttered Baz, pulling the rug around them.

'Bet you haven't got a safety pin,' joked Sumo.

Baz grinned and pulled something out of his pocket.

'I've got a sort of one,' he said and fastened the rug securely with his lucky charm – the cannibal chief's iron false teeth!

'Chief Bellibungful bites again,' he joked.

'Magic!' chuckled Sumo. 'You make a smashing pet, Baz!'

'Cheeky!' said Baz and they were just starting a play fight when there was the sound of a key turning in the front door lock.

Baz tensed and nudged Sumo.

'This is *it*. And *no* funny business! If you goof this one up, you've lost Hedda for good!'

Sumo's eyeballs nodded on their stalks. 'You got it, Baz,' he whispered. 'No funny business.'

Chapter 17

A lead balloon

The front door creaked open. Footsteps entered the lobby and stopped. Baz and Sumo waited for a reaction. There was none.

Professor Fogeldurge walked slowly out of the lobby and into the canteen. No reaction. He moved through the exhibits and past the accusing headlines like a sleepwalker.

He turned silently into his office. He unlocked the safe and lifted out Hedda's skull.

Baz felt Sumo tense next to him.

'Remember – no funny business!' he whispered.

The Professor laid Hedda's skull down on his desk. He looked up and his grim, grey face twisted into a mask of fury. He had come face to face with Queen Wannabee the First, mouldering away in his office chair.

It was the Queen who broke the spell. The Professor threw a mega wobbler. His museum had been vandalized – wrecked – trashed! He was livid! He was furious – but he didn't make a sound.

Instead, he pulled his big hat off his head and started to chew it. Then he tossed the hat onto his desk, grabbed a stuffed toad from a shelf and set about chewing that instead. He gnawed the edge of his desk and finished off with several scrunched-up paper balls.

And he did it all in total silence.

He looked really comical, but it wasn't funny at all. Baz had expected him to blow his top and make such a rumpus that people would come to see what was up. But nobody would hear anything because there was nothing to hear.

Baz suddenly remembered the business with Hoots McToot's bagpipes. Professor Fogeldurge couldn't stand loud noises.

'Well, that went down like a lead balloon,' whispered Sumo.

They lay motionless under the grizzly bearskin and watched.

The Professor picked up his hat, straightened the chewed brim and put it back on. He felt more in charge of things when he had his hat firmly clamped down on his shiny pink head.

He picked up Hedda's skull and smiled a crafty smile.

'So, my dear, someone knows about my little business,' he said to her. 'Never mind, we can easily get round it. I'll lock this place up so no one else can snoop around. Then you and I will do the deal with His ex-Majesty. After that, I'll fly off to a place in the sun and never be seen again. The cash I'll get for you, my pretty, will keep me in luxury for the rest of my life.'

Sumo lay in a miserable ball under the rug.

'Nobody's come. The plan isn't working, Baz! Nothing's going to stop him selling Hedda. I've got to do something ... ' And to Baz's horror, Sumo began to slither away.

'Where do you think you're going?' hissed Baz.

Sumo stared at him. He looked oh so serious.

'I'm going home,' he said. 'Wherever Hedda goes, I go. Thanks for having me as your pet, Baz. It's been fun.' Then he slid silently across the corridor and disappeared into Professor Fogeldurge's den.

Baz watched him going. He felt helpless and hopeless. The plan hadn't worked. Nobody had come. Sumo was sure to be spotted; his pet was about to become his ex-pet.

Through the open office door, Baz could see the Professor frantically shredding papers. They were probably evidence of his shady deals.

As he watched, he saw Queen Wannabee the First suddenly twitch. It was Sumo, slithering through her tatty hair. He did a nifty shimmy into her nostrils, only to reappear out of a hole where her thumb had once been. He came out right next to Hedda.

He slithered up into Hedda's eye socket and, turning towards Baz, he waved his eyestalks, winked and slipped inside. Sumo had gone home.

Chapter 18

Curry-coloured earwax

Baz jumped – someone had come into the entrance lobby. Whoever it was started to laugh.

'Hey, come and look at this,' she called. 'There's this crazy knight sitting on a totem pole with a potty on his head!'

Feet clattered into the lobby, followed by a gale of hoots and giggles. A crowd of teenagers wandered into the corridor and gazed around in amazement.

'You know what – this is almost cool.'

Under the bearskin rug, Baz was smiling. The plan was working, at last.

He heard the office door close quietly. Professor Fogeldurge had gone to ground.

'I fancy a date with the gladiator,' one of the girls giggled.

'No chance. You'd have to settle for one of the headless guys,' somebody joked.

'Quit fooling around, you lot!' a boy interrupted. 'There's some really crazy stuff written on the walls over here and a sort of a trail on the floor.' And he started to follow Sumo's arrows.

'Come and have a look at this!' he shouted.

They clustered round Sumo's Skull Sluggery Breaking Nooze on the wall above the fake talking skull of Princess Hedda of Defunctovia.

'There's something weird going on around here,' he said and they all stared into the glass case.

'Read the blurb,' said one of them.

There was a brief silence while they took it in.

'Go on then,' said the boy. 'Push the button!'

'Who dares to disturb the sleep of Princess Hedda of Defunctovia? May verrucas sprout between your toes and spiders live inside your nose!' chanted the MP3 player.

'Let's see what this Fogeldurge guy has to say for himself,' said one of the girls and they marched off towards the office.

Bang! She punched the door.

'Excuse us, Professor,' she called. 'We'd like a word with you.'

No reply.

'Is it true that you're faking things here in the museum?' she went on.

No reply.

'He's not in,' she shrugged.

At that moment, there came the sound of laughter in the lobby.

'What the heck's that chap in armour doing up the pole?' chuckled a man.

'I think it's what they call modern art,' said a woman, and in came a group of pensioners. They made a beeline for the jukebox.

'I haven't seen one of these since I was sixteen,' said the woman. 'See if it works, Reg.'

Reg twiddled the dials. Lights flashed, an arm dropped a record onto the turntable and 'We're gonna rock around the clock tonight!' belted out through the museum.

Walking sticks, flat caps and woolly cardigans were tossed aside as the pensioners jived, bopped and twisted, and sang along with the record.

'Show us how to do that,' said one of the teenagers, and the frumpy old museum throbbed to the fifties beat.

Inside the office, Professor Fogeldurge had his hands clamped over his ears.

'Shut up! I can't stand it! I have very delicate hearing. I've got to get out of here!' And, muttering something about curry-coloured earwax, he flung the office door open.

Out zipped Professor Fogeldurge, with his large hat pulled firmly down on his large head. He was making a run for it.

Chapter 19
The skullnapper

Professor Fogeldurge's bandy little legs sprinted for the door.

Baz struggled to his feet.

'Stop him!' he yelled.

'Aah!' screamed an elderly woman, pointing wildly at Baz. 'It's a grizzly!'

'No, I'm not!' snapped Baz.

'It's a *talking* grizzly!' shouted Reg. He snatched the crocodile puppet from Bashius Maximus and shook it threateningly at Baz. 'Stay back, you monster – I'm armed!'

'Oh, forget it,' groaned Baz. There was no time to explain.

He dashed into the museum office – Hedda's skull had gone.

'Listen! You've got to believe me,' he pleaded with the visitors. 'That skull in the case is a fake. Professor Fogeldurge is going to sell the genuine one – like now!' And he bolted out of the museum.

'I'm with you, little fella,' shouted Reg, scuttling after him.

'I was a wrestler! I'll sort him!' shouted an elderly lady and she scampered after Reg.

'What are we waiting for?' exclaimed one of the girls. 'If they can play catch the crook – so can we!' The excited bunch of teenagers charged outside.

Up the street ran the grizzly bear, with half a dozen pensioners and a gaggle of teenagers hot on his heels. The problem was that no one outside of the museum knew what was happening. It looked as if a crowd of people were chasing a bear.

'I'll get the grizzly!' yelled a woman and she netted Baz's furry head in a huge shopping bag.

'Gerroff!' he growled and yanked the bag off his head.

Shopping-Bag-Woman was joined by a whole herd of shoppers who were chasing the teenagers, who were chasing the pensioners, who were chasing Baz, who was chasing the skullnapper.

The town was in chaos.

The town clock stood at two minutes to noon as the Quidsin Bank came into sight. The deal between Blingking Dud and the Professor would be over in two minutes.

Baz put on a spurt – it was now or never!

He hurtled towards the impressive building. The automatic doors purred open and he stumbled inside. There was a shemozzle[15] as the pensioners, the teenagers and the shoppers all piled in behind him.

'Call the police,' hissed Shopping-Bag-Woman. 'The grizzly's robbing the bank!'

Within seconds, the switchboard at the local police station was working on overload.

Baz scanned the queues for a small man in a very big hat and a tall man with a lot of bling. It wasn't easy to see through the bear's jaws, but he was sure that they weren't there. Then ...

'They're not in the quooze, Baz,' called a muffled voice.

Baz spun around – and there they were! Professor Fogeldurge and Blingking Dud were skulking behind a marble pillar and Dud was handing over a bulging bag. But where was Hedda?

'Stop that man!' Baz shouted. 'He's a skullnapper!'

He cringed, realizing too late how daft that must have sounded. Nobody would have the foggiest idea what a skullnapper was.

Professor Fogeldurge smirked at the crowd.

'The boy's a joker,' he told them.

---

[15] commotion

Baz groaned. They were all staring at him and muttering. They obviously thought that he'd been playing the fool. He'd blown it.

It was then that the police arrived with a wail of sirens and a flash of blue lights.

'Arrest that Grizzly,' demanded Shopping-Bag-Woman, but the police ignored her.

There were three of them; one was a chief inspector, one was his sergeant and the other one was …

'Aunt Enna!' gasped Baz.

'How very confoozing,' chortled a voice.

No funny business please, Sumo, thought Baz.

Aunt Enna scanned the huge marble hall. Her gaze fell on the grizzly bear.

'Oh, there you are, Baz,' she said, as if it was perfectly natural to find her nephew in a posh bank, dressed in a bearskin. 'Which one do you want arresting?'

Baz pushed the grizzly's head back like a hood.

'Professor Fogeldurge,' he stated firmly.

'On what charge? ' snorted the Professor.

'On the charge of kidnapping an ancient skull,' said the Inspector.

'Hey, I want out of this!' growled Blingking Dud, grabbing the money bag back. 'I'm ex-King Dudley of Defunctovia. I don't do dodgy deals!'

'And neither do I!' exclaimed Professor Fogeldurge. 'I have no idea what they're talking about!'

The policemen searched the Professor's bag and his pockets and found absolutely nothing.

'But – he *has* to have it!' protested Baz. 'He was going to do the deal here at noon.'

The Inspector looked embarrassed. 'I'm sorry, sir,' he apologized to the Professor. 'We must have received unreliable information.'

'That's perfectly all right, Inspector,' beamed Professor Fogeldurge. 'I bid you good day.' And with his usual good manners, he bowed and, without thinking, he lifted his hat!

Oops! Professor Fogeldurge froze.

There, sitting on the top of his bald, pink head, was Hedda's skull!

Everyone watched, mesmerized, as a revolting black dollop squirmed out of one of her eye sockets and dangled in front of the Professor's eyes.

'Gotcha, dude!' said the black dollop gleefully.

Chapter 20

The diamond geezer

And so it was over. Here was Baz, back in the kitchen where it had all started, with Aunt Enna rummaging around in the freezer.

'Chief Bellibungful's false teeth have gone missing,' she said.

'No they haven't,' said Baz, pulling them out of his pocket. 'They were my good luck charm.'

Aunt Enna raised her eyebrows.

'You're full of surprises, Baz Boston,' she smiled. 'I had no idea that you were carrying out a master plan in the Dumpsdown Museum.'

'And I had no idea that you were a secret agent!' he retorted.

'Oh, nothing so glamorous,' she laughed. 'I was just giving the police a bit of help. They suspected that Professor Fogeldurge was up to something shady, but they had nothing to pin him down.'

'Well, they've got plenty now,' grinned Baz.

'Yes. Hedda's skull is just the latest in a very long line of dodgy deals.'

She picked up a hunk of cheese and absent-mindedly

started to grate it with Chief Bellibungful's false teeth.

'Aunt Enna,' Baz began, 'there's somebody I'd like you to meet.'

He went up to his room. It was time for his aunt to meet his pet ...

Aunt Enna looked confused when Baz reappeared in the kitchen holding Hedda's skull.

'But I know Hedda already,' she pointed out.

'Yes, but you haven't met her lodger ...'

'Yoo-hoo,' called a voice and an eyeball winked out of one of Hedda's eye sockets, followed by the rest of Sumo's impressive bulk. 'Hello there, clever Auntie.'

Aunt Enna kept her cool. She had seen lots of oozy animals in her line of work, but nothing quite so oozy – or quite so lippy – as this one.

'Hello, er ...'

'The name's Sumo!' beamed Sumo. 'But you can call me Diamond Geezer.'

She turned to Baz. 'OK, let's settle this once and for all, Baz. Are you throwing your voice? Yes or no?'

'No,' he said seriously.

'So who's doing the talking?' she asked.

'Sumo is.'

'Say something else,' she told Sumo.

'I'm Baz's pet. Hedda's my historic home. And I want it to stay that way!' gabbled Sumo.

Aunt Enna thought for a moment and then nodded. 'All right,' she said, 'so we don't have a talking skull. What we *do* have is a talking slug!'

'Yes,' agreed Baz.

'OK, I'm cool with all of that,' said his aunt. 'Now, tell me all about your crook-catching adventures. I guess I'm in for a lot more surprises.'

She was ...

'It's a shame about the Dumpsdown Museum,' said Aunt Enna a few days later. 'The police have taken everything away as evidence and the whole place is empty. It's such a waste of space and look at us – we're full to bursting with all my dig-ups.'

'You could open your own museum ... ' smiled Baz.

Load by load, Aunt Enna's dig-ups were transferred to the Dumpsdown Museum.

'We've got to make this place really exciting, Baz,' she said.

'And don't forget the Prime-Time-Slime Interaction,' grinned Sumo.

Lorries rolled up, loaded with Aunt Enna's bizarre finds. The jumbo dig-ups from the garden all had their place, even the massive stone statue of the cross-eyed god with the bushy green bogies.

'We need a new name,' said Aunt Enna. 'Dumpsdown sounds like a rubbish tip.'

'What about *Antenna's Arty Facts*?' suggested Sumo.

'Perfect!' she laughed. 'You're a brilliant pet, Sumo.'

Sumo looked smug and inflated himself to full stretch.

Baz stared at him. 'You're putting weight on!' he said.

'Tosh!' said Sumo and slithered into Hedda's eye socket, but half way in, he stopped.

'Hey, Baz!' he spluttered. Hedda's shrunk!'

'Skulls don't shrink,' said Baz. 'I told you before, you've put weight on.'

‘Tiddley-push!’ snorted Sumo, but no matter how much he wiggled and waggled, he couldn’t get through the eye socket.

‘I’m just a young’un,’ he said. ‘I guess I’ve still got a lot of growing to do. So I’ve lost my historic home after all,’ he chuntered and curled up around Baz’s shoulders in a long, oozy splodge.

‘Maybe not,’ said Baz thoughtfully. ‘Come on. Let’s go house hunting!’ And grabbing Hedda’s skull and his skateboard, they sped through town towards Antenna’s Arty Facts.

‘What you need is a historic home with mega attitude,’ Baz told Sumo as they made their way through the dig-ups in the museum. ‘So how about that one?’ and he pointed to the huge stone statue of the cross-eyed god with the mossy, green bogies.

‘Oh, wow!’ gasped Sumo. ‘When do I move in?’

‘How about now?’ smiled Baz. ‘And Hedda’s skull can move in with you.’

Out of nowhere, a little voice said, ‘Thanks guys. You’re the biz!’

They stared in astonishment at Hedda’s skull.

‘I didn’t say that!’ said Baz.

'*I* didn't say that!' said Sumo.

The Antenna's Arty Facts Museum was a rip-roaring success. People were wowed by the magical, madcap exhibits, they marvelled at the weird and wonderful art and the Prime-Time-Slime Interaction was a big hit. But best of all was swapping ooze jokes with the mysterious, talking statue of the huge, cross-eyed god.

The god didn't seem to mind about being the historic home of an oversized slug. Hidden behind its cross-eyed windows, Sumo cheerily slithered through the vast airy spaces. Baz had told him that slugs have ninety thousand grandchildren, so he had to find them all bedrooms. They would need plenty of veggie grub, but Sumo had that sussed. Growing in the god's huge nostrils was an endless supply of mossy, green bogies!

About the author

I live in the North East of England where the friendly people, the lively towns and the wild, open countryside really spark off the imagination. My house is in a wooded valley so I get to meet a lot of slugs! It was them that gave me the idea for this book.

Writing fiction is exciting, especially when new characters arrive in my mind and a new story begins. I also write non-fiction, and have written about finding dodgy dig-ups, like skeletons, in the garden!